Cowardly Howard

'Cowardly Howard'
An original concept by Katie Dale
© Katie Dale 2024

Illustrated by Denis Alonso

Published by MAVERICK ARTS PUBLISHING LTD
Suite 1, Hillreed House, 54 Queen Street,
Horsham, West Sussex, RH13 5AD
© Maverick Arts Publishing Limited August 2024
+44 (0)1403 256941

A CIP catalogue record for this book is available at the British Library.

ISBN 978-1-83511-026-?

Printed in India

www.maverickbooks.co.uk

London Borough of Enfield	
91200000823355	
Askews & Holts	18-Oct-2024
JF YGN BEGINNER READE	
ENSOUT	

This book is rated as: Orange Band (Guided Reading)
It follows the requirements for Phase 5 phonics.
Most words are decodable, and any non-decodable words are familiar, supported by the context and/or represented in the artwork.

Cowardly Howard

By Katie Dale

Illustrated by Denis Alonso

Howard was big!

Howard was strong!

But...

Most days he hid in his barn.

But even in there he got scared!

Then one day, Buttercup arrived.

"Hi!" she called. Howard hid.

"I LOVE hide and seek!" Buttercup giggled.

Howard kept as quiet as a mouse...

But then he saw a mouse!

"Found you!" Buttercup cried.

"What were you scared of?"

Howard pointed at the mouse.

"It might bite me!"

Buttercup smiled. "He won't bite! Come out, little mouse!"

Howard hid behind Buttercup as the mouse crept fearfully out.

Howard smiled.

Maybe Buttercup was right.

Howard hid.

"It's just the wind," Buttercup said.

"It won't hurt you."

"Are you s-sure?" Howard stammered.

"Come outside," Buttercup said.

Howard smiled.

Buttercup was right.

"Were you scared of me too?" Buttercup asked.

Howard nodded. "I was afraid you wouldn't like me."

"I do like you!" Buttercup smiled.

"I was scared you didn't like me, because you hid!"

"I like you very much,"

Howard said, beaming.

But the next day, Buttercup had vanished!

Was she playing hide and seek again?

Howard looked everywhere.

Howard took a deep breath. "Have you seen Buttercup?" he asked bravely. "She's been taken to the next field!" the bunny said.

Howard set off for the fence but there was mucky mud...

...a wobbly log...

...and sticky cobwebs.

Howard started running back to his barn. But then he remembered what Buttercup had said.

"They won't hurt me," he told himself.

Howard took a deep breath, then...

he tiptoed through the mucky mud.

He wibbled over the wobbly log...

...and pushed through the sticky cobwebs.

Until...

"Howard!" Buttercup cried happily. "You came all this way to find me? Weren't you scared?"

"Yes," Howard admitted. "But...

"...I was more afraid that I would never see you again." Howard said. "That was the scariest thing of all."

"You never need to fear that," Buttercup smiled. "We'll be friends forever."

Quiz

1. Howard was big! Howard was…
a) strong!
b) scared!
c) shy!

2. Where does Howard hide most days?
a) The field
b) The mud
c) The barn

3. What does Buttercup tell Howard about the mouse he is afraid of?
a) He's only small!
b) He's more scared of you!
c) He's not going to hurt you!

Book Bands for Guided Reading

The Institute of Education book banding system is a scale of colours that reflects the various levels of reading difficulty. The bands are assigned by taking into account the content, the language style, the layout and phonics. Word, phrase and sentence level work is also taken into consideration.

Maverick Early Readers are a bright, attractive range of books covering the pink to white bands. All of these books have been book banded for guided reading to the industry standard and edited by a leading educational consultant.

To view the whole Maverick Readers scheme, visit our website at www.maverickearlyreaders.com

Or scan the QR code above to view our scheme instantly!

Quiz Answers: 1a, 2c, 3b, 4a, 5c

4. Who pops up out of the ground?
a) A bunny
b) A worm
c) A squirrel

5. When Howard can't find Buttercup, where has she gone?
a) The barn
b) The muddy park
c) The next field

Turn over for answers